COWGIRL MEGAN
by Trisha Magraw

Illustrations by
Janîce Leotti

Spot Illustrations by
Rich Grote

MAGIC ATTIC PRESS

As members of the
MAGIC ATTIC CLUB,
we promise to
be best friends,
share all of our adventures in the attic,
use our imaginations,
have lots of fun together,
and remember—the real magic is in us.

Alison   *Keisha*

Heather   *Megan*

Table of Contents

Chapter

One

THE SURPRISE VISITOR

Megan brushed her hair quickly, then stuffed her sweaty gym clothes into the bright green canvas bag that Aunt Frances had given her last Christmas.

"If we're late for class, we're going to blame you," kidded Heather as she passed Megan, slamming the door to the girls' locker room on her way out.

Heather Hardin was one of Megan's best friends. She

knew Heather would wait for her on the bench in the lobby. So would Keisha Vance and Alison McCann. The bench just outside the gym door was one of the regular spots where the girls met. Whenever they said "our bench," everybody knew exactly what they meant.

Sure enough, when Megan pushed through the gym doors, her friends were crowded together at one end, their books and gym clothes in three piles on the floor.

"Okay, I'm ready!" cried Megan. But Alison, Heather, and Keisha were so busy talking that none of them even looked up.

"What's going on?" asked Megan.

"The surprise guest," replied Alison. "We're all making guesses about who it's going to be."

The day before, their teacher, Ms. Austin, had announced that instead of Language Arts, someone would speak to the class. Ms. Austin hadn't told them who it would be. She said she wanted to surprise the class.

Ms. Austin was one of the most popular teachers at Lincoln School, partly because she could make even the hardest assignments seem like fun. Her latest idea was to invite people from the community to tell their class about their real-life experiences.

"I'll bet it's the woman biologist from Community College who's in training to become an astronaut," suggested Heather. "My mom was reading me an article from the paper about her the other day."

"I don't think that's it," said Alison. "Not unless astronauts use long ropes. I saw a rope rolled up under Ms. Austin's desk, and some other stuff. . . ."

"I know!" cried Keisha. "It's her dog, Little Junior! What you saw is his extra-long leash. She's been looking for an excuse to bring him to class." Everybody laughed.

"Come on," cried Megan over the noise of the warning bell. "There's only one way to find out." So the four girls grabbed their things and headed down the corridor to class. They arrived just seconds before the final bell. The room was quiet and most of the kids were already seated.

"Please take your seats quickly," Ms. Austin told the class cheerfully.

Right away, Megan noticed an athletic-looking woman sitting in a chair next to Ms. Austin's big desk. The woman seemed so young that she might have been a new student teacher. She reminded Megan of a swimming coach she'd had one summer. She had short brown hair, curly and pushed behind her ears. Her khaki pants and white T-shirt were casual, but her open navy blue blazer had a flowered scarf tucked in the pocket. When Megan took a closer look, she could read the lettering on the guest's T-shirt. It said, "MAKE THE MOUNTAIN" in bright orange letters. Megan wondered what that meant. . . .

Then Megan noticed that the woman wore heavy hiking boots. They looked like the serious kind, not the popular leather boots that the kids in her class liked to wear every day.

Ms. Austin tapped the desk gently with her pencil. "Class, we're very privileged to have as our surprise guest today Ms. Hannah Green."

Hannah Green smiled as Ms. Austin pulled the coil of rope, a small pickax, and a pair of shoes with spiked soles from under the big desk.

"Guess I was wrong about Little Junior," whispered Keisha, who sat right behind Megan.

Megan tried hard not to giggle.

"Some of you may have guessed that Hannah Green is a mountain climber. An expert mountain climber." Ms. Austin added, "she has taken part in climbing competitions throughout the country and is outstanding in her field. Or perhaps I should say on her mountains. . . ."

Ms. Austin's joke was corny, but the class broke into laughter anyway.

"But Hannah Green is more than that," Ms. Austin continued, more seriously. "She is an expert as well at many other things. . . ." Ms. Austin paused and nodded to Hannah Green. "I'll let her tell you the rest."

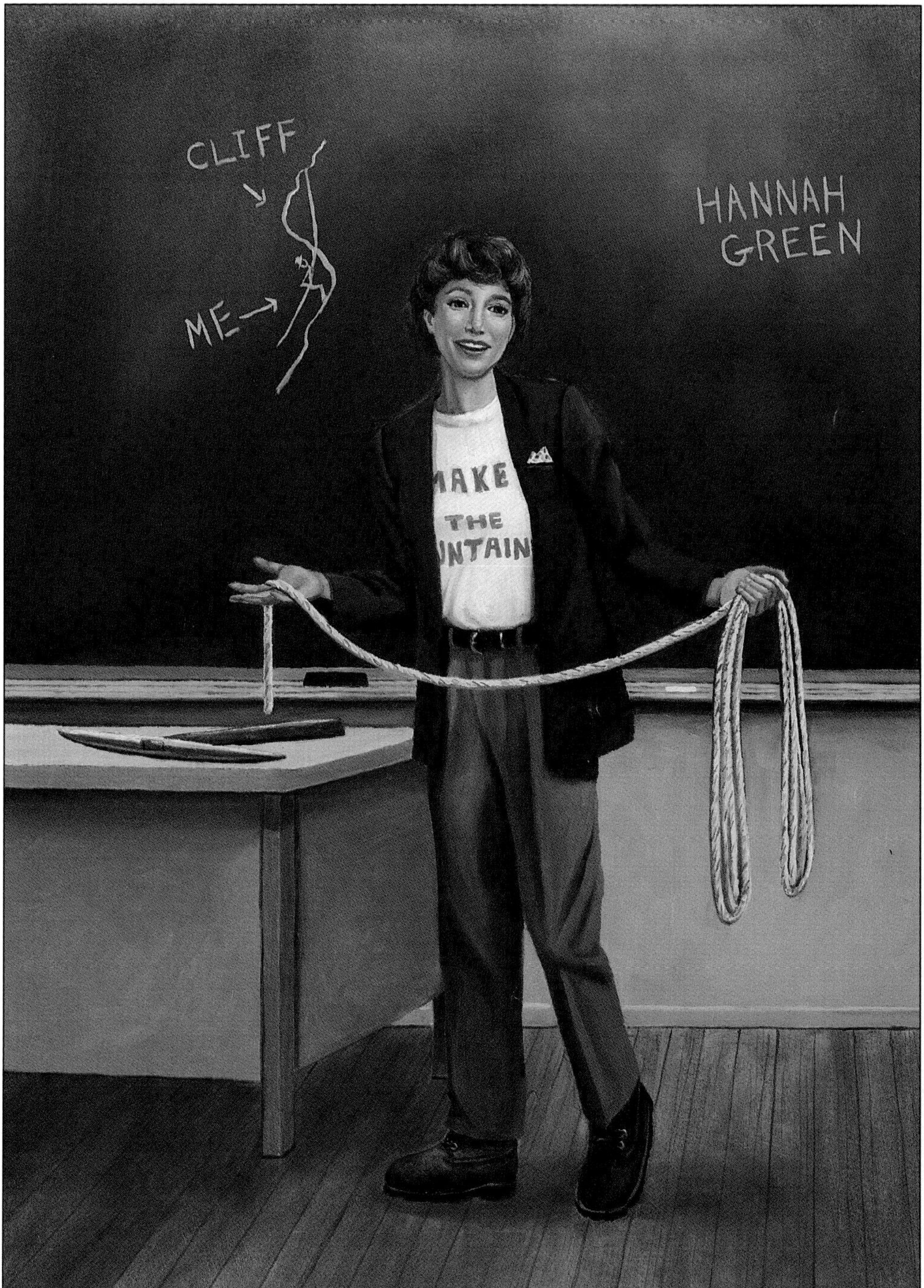
CLIFF
ME
HANNAH
GREEN

With that, Ms. Austin walked to the back of the room, where she slipped into an empty desk chair. The class clapped politely as Ms. Green rose from her chair by the desk.

"Hello," said Ms. Green warmly. "Well, you know who I am now. And this . . ." Hannah Green reached for the rope on the desk. "This is my lifeline." She pointed to the other items on the desk. "And these are the tools of my trade."

For the next twenty minutes, nobody whispered, nobody doodled in their notebooks, nobody even yawned. Hannah Green kept everybody spellbound. She told the class it had been her lifelong dream to look at the earth from its highest points. She talked about skill, danger, and daring. Her adventures scaling cliffs and bounding off rocky mountainsides sounded like something they'd seen on the news or on some wilderness program.

Megan held her breath when Ms. Green began describing a move she once used to get out of an especially difficult spot on a steep ledge high above the ground.

"Here, I'll draw it for you," she said, glancing over her shoulder at the blackboard. "It will be easier to understand my predicament."

Ms. Green turned to walk over to the blackboard. It was no more than ten feet from her chair, but she walked stiffly and with great difficulty. Megan could tell that beneath her long pants Hannah Green wore a leg brace. Megan knew then that the expert mountain climber Hannah Green had a physical disability.

"I'll bet you're surprised I didn't zip right over to the blackboard," said Hannah Green frankly. "Everything your teacher told you about my skill as a mountain climber is true. But what she didn't tell you is that my climbing requires a little extra skill."

Megan still couldn't believe her eyes. For the next couple of minutes, she tried hard not to stare at Hannah Green's leg. She found herself looking away when Ms. Green dropped the chalk on the floor and nearly lost her balance when she stooped to pick it up. Megan wondered if she should have jumped up and gotten the chalk for her. It was hard to know just how to act.

Megan tried to catch Alison's eye from across the room. But Alison was tapping her eraser uneasily on her desk. Then Megan felt Keisha poke her in the middle of the back. It would be impolite to turn around, so she looked straight ahead.

"I asked your teacher not to tell you all this ahead of time because my handicap is simply one part of who I am. I'm not a handicapped mountain climber. I'm a mountain climber, and I happen to have a handicap that I have worked hard to overcome. There's a difference."

Megan liked the way Hannah Green was so open and honest. By the end of the class, she had almost forgotten about Ms. Green's handicap.

"I know most of you have read my T-shirt." Ms. Green laughed and held open her jacket. "MAKE THE MOUNTAIN!" She repeated each word carefully. "That simple little motto has gotten me through some tough times."

Ms. Green seemed to be smiling right at Megan when she added, "It's not just for mountain climbers, you know. I hope you'll all tuck the words in a safe place in your heads."

Chapter Two

DREAMS

hat do you think happened to her?" Alison wondered.

"I guess we could have asked her," replied Megan. "I thought it was great the way she talked about everything."

"Most of my mom's patients with disabilities don't want other people feeling sorry for them," said Keisha, whose mother was a nurse.

Megan and her friends were sitting on the porch in front of Heather's house, drinking frosty bottles of orange juice before they had to head home for dinner.

"I'd really like to learn to be that good at mountain climbing," said Alison. "Hannah Green's the best, too, physical disability or no physical disability."

"She made me feel like I could do anything," declared Heather. "Even my English homework."

All four girls groaned. They had just started writing short free verse for a poetry unit. The first assignment had sounded so simple when Ms. Austin instructed the class, "I want you to get to the point quickly. Be brief and surprising," but not even Megan, who loved English and was really smart in school, got it right at first.

"I finally found a way to make the poetry assignments easier," Megan told her friends. "Just write about something you like or something that means a lot to you."

"Give us a hint," said Alison.

"Okay," Megan went on. "Last night I wrote one that goes like this:

> Dream world becomes real.
> Dreams are me.
> Wait for me, world!"

"Not bad," said Keisha. "What does it mean?"

"It's about all the things I dream about doing when I'm older. It's about wanting to become a famous diplomat some day," Megan said, confiding in her friends. "You know, somebody who represents her government to other countries."

"You mean like the people your father gets to interview?" asked Heather.

"Right," replied Megan, whose father was a foreign correspondent. He traveled around the world and wrote articles about all kinds of famous people.

"Wow, you've got some pretty big ideas!" exclaimed Keisha while raising one eyebrow.

"What do you mean?" asked Megan, surprised at the doubt in Keisha's voice.

"Let's be realistic," said Keisha. "Not many people get to be diplomats."

"I know," said Megan firmly. "But that doesn't mean I shouldn't try. Everybody likes it when I head up school projects, so maybe I'll be good at leadership when I get older."

"Yeah," added Alison. "You were a great director when we gave our performance of *Peter Pan* that time for the senior citizens, but that doesn't mean you can take on the whole world!"

Megan felt she had to defend herself. "Remember when Hannah Green said a lot of people told her she couldn't climb mountains and she refused to listen?"

"Well, that's different," said Alison. "That's about overcoming a handicap."

"It's not different, and you're not being fair!"

"Fair or unfair, how are you going to be away so much if you have a family?" asked Heather.

"My mom has always worked," declared Megan, whose mother was a successful lawyer.

"Yeah, but she doesn't fly off to jobs in South America or Australia," replied Alison. "She can get home in a hurry."

"My dad flies all over the place." Megan did wish her father were around more often. Still, he never let his work stand in his way where she was concerned.

"I can see wanting to have an exciting job," said Heather, "but maybe you ought to pick something a little more realistic."

Megan couldn't believe her ears. "Forget it," she told her friends as she gathered up her books. "I wish I'd never brought it up."

When Megan got home, she dropped her backpack by the front door. As she passed the hall table, she spotted a colorful brochure about a dude ranch addressed to her. There was a girl her age on the cover, riding an adorable brown pony with a white splash down his face. Lucky girl! thought Megan.

Megan thumbed through the brochure, wondering who

had sent it to her. Probably her father. He knew she loved
to read about the Old West. She had read practically
every book about Annie Oakley and Buffalo Bill, the
famous Wild West Show performers. Her father also knew
how much Megan loved horses, and how much she
wished she could have a horse of her own.

"That you?" Aunt Frances called from the kitchen.
Megan could hear her setting the table.

"Hey, look what I found," said Megan, waving the dude
ranch brochure at her aunt.

Aunt Frances folded the napkins and put them next to the plates. Then, suddenly, she began to chuckle to herself.

"What's so funny?" Megan wanted to know.

"I was just remembering how you asked your parents for a pony for Christmas every year when you were little. It was always written in big letters at the top of your list. You tried to convince everyone that a small pony would fit quite comfortably in the garage."

"I still dream about having a horse out back," admitted Megan, smiling, "but I know it's a wild kind of dream."

"That's called a pipe dream," said Aunt Frances, "an unrealistic kind of dream."

"Is being an international diplomat a pipe dream?" Megan wanted to know.

"If you put your mind to it, you can be anything you want to be," replied Aunt Frances. "Being a diplomat doesn't sound like a pipe dream. Not like keeping a pony in the garage."

"That's what I think," Megan told Aunt Frances. "I just wish my friends understood."

Dreams

Megan looked at the clock in the kitchen. She had plenty of time before her mother got home. Her homework was mostly finished and the poetry was easy now, so that wouldn't take much time.

"I'm going over to Ellie's," Megan told her aunt. Ellie Goodwin, a colorful and friendly older woman, lived near Megan. Ellie had recently moved back into her family's big Victorian house, which came to life with her many incredible souvenirs from travels around the world. It was there that Megan, Heather, Keisha, and Alison had started the Magic Attic Club.

Thinking about what her friends had said, Megan knew she needed to go to Ellie's, if only for a little while, to be alone in the attic.

"Don't lose track of the time," cautioned Aunt Frances.

"I won't," Megan promised.

As she headed out the kitchen door, Megan spotted her cat Ginger sitting on the windowsill, catching the last rays of the setting sun.

"Howdy, pardner," mocked Megan in her best western drawl.

Ginger just yawned.

Chapter
Three

HEADING WEST

"Yoo hoo!" Ellie called from the yard as Megan rounded the corner of her house. Monty, Ellie's energetic terrier, dashed across the yard to greet Megan.

"Some guard dog you are," she told Monty as he licked her hand.

Ellie was kneeling in a flower bed, a soft wide-brimmed hat shading her from the late afternoon sun. Dozens of spring flowers were popping up all over the beautiful big yard.

"I had forgotten how many bulbs I planted last fall!" declared Ellie, taking a deep breath and removing her pink garden gloves.

"I was wondering . . ." Megan began.

"I'll bet I know just what you're wondering," replied Ellie brightly, pushing back a loose strand of hair. "Now let me keep at these stubborn weeds before I'm gardening in the dark."

"Thanks," said Megan as she headed for the front door and the hallway where she knew she would find the key in the silver box. Then she walked quickly up the stairs and on up to the attic.

Sometimes Megan spent a long time looking at each outfit, holding the separate pieces up to the mirror. This time was a little different, maybe because of the dude ranch brochure or the talk about wanting a pony in the garage. Megan went right to a white western hat hanging on a tall wooden rack. It was as though the hat had been waiting just for her. When she put it on her head, it fit perfectly.

The outfit that matched was in the steamer trunk, right on top. Colorful rhinestones and gold-colored

studs—shaped like small circles and stars—decorated it. They glittered when Megan took the jacket, top, and skirt from the trunk. Quickly, she slipped into the clothes, then pulled on a pair of handsome white leather boots. The outfit was complete.

Megan stood in front of the long mirror, turning this way and that to see herself from all sides. She loved the way her every move made the gold fringe on the jacket dance. Now all I need is a horse, she thought excitedly.

The western clothes made Megan feel like a real cowgirl, and her eyes began to shine. She held up her arms, grasping an invisible pair of reins. "Whoa!" she cried in the quiet of the attic, pulling back hard on make-believe reins.

When Megan glanced into the mirror again, the rhinestones on her jacket sparkled so brightly that she had to look away. She looked down at the western boots. They looked brand new, but something was different. . . .

Megan looked again and saw that her white leather boots were covered with dust!

"Hold him, cowgirl! Wrangle him in!" a man's deep voice shouted. Suddenly, Megan realized the directions were intended for her.

Megan felt a tug on her arms and looked up. She was in the middle of a dusty corral. The wide open spaces and the mountains in the distance told her she was somewhere in the West. The constant tugging told Megan she'd better do exactly as the cowboy said, because a frisky horse was at the other end of the rope she held.

Megan tightened her hold and the horse began to let up.

"Show him you mean business!" the same voice shouted again. The tall cowboy was watching Megan's every move. He whipped off his black hat and slapped it against his jeans.

"Hey, Sam! Sam Duffey!" a couple of cowboys shouted from the far side of the corral in a good-natured way. "Looks like you got a wild one there!" Sam Duffey laughed and waved at the men.

Right away Megan could tell that these were real cowboys. Their clothes were muddy and worn, and they had spurs on their high leather boots. Others nearby on horseback had heavy leather chaps strapped over their jeans. Megan knew from her western books that only serious riders wore chaps for protection. Most of the men wore their bandanas with the tie in the back. Out west, you pulled the bandana over your mouth when the wind blew hot and dusty.

"Nothing we can't handle, this cowgirl and me," Sam Duffey replied evenly as if nothing shook him. He laughed again, but he never took his eyes off Megan and the spirited horse for a second. Megan's mom called people like Sam Duffey "unflappable."

Megan knew Sam was the boss, the head wrangler, from the respectful way the others treated him. Sam walked closer, carrying a leather halter. His strong but gentle presence made the horse calm down right away. "Good boy," soothed Sam, coming closer and stroking his neck. "Let's slip this on you."

Megan still couldn't believe it. The horse was real! He was the softest shade of brown—like caramel candy—with bold patches of white. His thick white mane matched his equally thick tail, and he was ten times more beautiful than the horse on the dude ranch brochure.

"I think he trusts you," said Megan, noticing how quiet the horse had become. She wondered how she'd ever handle him on her own. A horse was a cowboy's transportation, livelihood, and friend. Breaking in a new one was serious business.

"Trust is earned," replied Sam.

"What do you think I should do now?" asked Megan, hoping she'd get some hint from Sam about her role in this new adventure.

"Time's getting tight," Sam stated in his no-nonsense way, gesturing to the big ring nearby. "Soon this place is going to get turned into the biggest little wild west show around these parts. You've only got a few hours to get Thunderbolt under control."

Thunderbolt! thought Megan. Here I finally have the horse of my dreams, and he's wild enough to be named Thunderbolt.

She must have looked terrified because Sam said, "You've got what it takes, young lady, to be the best at trick riding this year. Thunderbolt's just feeling his oats. That happens. Let him know who's boss, and we'll have a new star of the wild west show by nightfall."

Sam gave Megan a friendly punch on the arm. Then he left her alone with Thunderbolt.

Trick riding. Wild west show. Thunderbolt was nibbling at the gold fringe on her jacket. How would she ever handle this one?

The noise in a big ring beyond the corral fence caught Megan's attention. Cowboys and cowgirls were busy practicing for the show. Dozens of horses and riders were working on their events at the same time. It seemed like a miracle that nobody was crashing into anyone.

A cheer went up as a cowboy came out of a chute on a bucking bronco. His arms and legs flew around like a rag doll out of control. Finally, the horse gave one powerful buck, and the cowboy flew off.

That could be me! thought Megan. But the cowboy picked himself up, dusted himself off, and walked out of the ring like nothing had happened. Megan laughed to herself. During the cowboy's wild ride, and even after he had gotten thrown, his hat stayed on.

A group of twenty cowgirls dressed in colorful spangled satin shirts took their horses around the ring at a brisk walk in groups of four. There was always a parade around the ring before the regular wild west show events—bronco busting, calf roping, and bull riding—and the crowd always clapped long and hard when the cowgirls rode in perfect step.

Megan felt a sudden jerk on the rope, different from the stubborn tugging. Thunderbolt again! Megan thought. She had been so busy watching all the things that were going on that she hadn't been paying attention to her horse. She hoped Sam Duffey hadn't seen her neglecting her job.

Now Thunderbolt was pulling hard, jerking at the rope and neighing loudly. Something had certainly spooked him, and he seemed determined to break away.

"Whoa!" cried Megan, hanging on with all her might.

Thunderbolt was getting more worked up. When he reared, Megan knew she was in trouble.

Megan thought her arms were going to be pulled from their sockets. The rope began to cut her hands, but she held on tight. If that cowboy could walk away from a bucking bronco, she could hold on to some horse.

"Hang on!" a voice cried. Somebody was coming up fast from behind. At first, Megan thought it was Sam. The accent was the same. But the voice was lighter and softer.

Then a hand reached out and gave a hard yank on the rope. Thunderbolt seemed to sense that the yank meant business. He settled down almost immediately.

Chapter
Four

THE NEW
FRIEND

Y ou okay?" asked the girl standing next to Megan.

"Yeah, thanks," mumbled Megan, embarrassed that somebody had to come to her rescue already.

"No problem," said the girl understandingly. "I'm happy to oblige. Besides, everybody knows Thunderbolt can be pretty frisky."

The girl moved her hand from the rope to Thunderbolt's neck. As she stroked the horse, he shook his head and settled down. Then she moved her hands down Thunderbolt's back, stopping in the middle.

"I *thought* he seemed a little harder to handle than usual," declared the girl flatly. "Bet he got stung by a bee. I think I feel a little raised spot. . . ."

"No wonder he tried to bolt!" cried Megan, feeling better that at least it wasn't all her fault.

Megan took a long look at the girl. They were about the same age, and about the same size. Their hair was a different color, Megan's a strawberry blond and the girl's a light brown. But with their big western hats on, it was hard to tell them apart.

"Thanks a lot," offered Megan. "You're really great with horses."

"Well, I am Kate *Duffey*," declared the girl, emphasizing her last name. Then she laughed and put out her hand to shake on it.

Kate was still holding out her hand, so Megan reached out, and the two girls shook hands. Kate had a strong handshake. She was not like anybody Megan had ever met before.

"How's your routine going?" asked Kate. "Pa told me

you're doing trick riding tonight." There was a sadness in Kate's voice that hadn't been there before. "I used to do that."

"What do you mean you *used* to?" asked Megan.

"I'm watching from the side this year," replied Kate. "So to speak," she added. Then she laughed in an odd way. Megan wondered if she had missed some joke.

A long stick was lying in the dust just a few feet away. Or was it the branch of a tree blown into the corral? When Megan took a better look, she could see it was a cane.

"Is that yours?" asked Megan, pointing to the cane.

"Is what mine?" asked Kate, looking straight ahead.

Kate didn't look at the cane. In fact, her gaze didn't seem focused on anything. Kate had *felt* Thunderbolt's back carefully. And Kate hadn't noticed when Megan didn't shake hands right away.

Megan realized that Kate Duffey was blind.

"I'll get your cane," said Megan, remembering what Mrs. Vance had told Keisha about not apologizing or feeling sorry for somebody who had a physical disability.

"I'd appreciate that," replied Kate.

Together, Megan and Kate walked Thunderbolt around the corral. Megan waited for Kate to use her cane, but she didn't seem to need it. She knew every inch of the corral. When they got to the gate, Kate warned Megan, "Watch

out for that new horse coming into the corral. Keep
Thunderbolt close."

Megan held Thunderbolt near the fence while a large
white horse passed them.

"That's Angel," Kate went on. "Don't let her name fool
you. She bites. Not people, but other horses. I think
Thunderbolt has had his share of bites today."

"You really do know everything that's going on, don't
you?" Megan asked Kate.

"Well, I might not be able to see, but I can hear better
and smell better than most people," Kate declared. Then
she laughed. "Angel's whinny is different from, say,
Thunderbolt's or Molly's or Lightning's. She also has a
heavy walk, and she smells like, well, she smells like
Angel! I can't explain better than that."

"That's really neat!" cried Megan.

"Well, I wish my father thought it was neat," Kate
blurted out.

"Why doesn't he?" asked Megan.

"It's a long story," groaned Kate.

"You mean about your blindness?" Megan asked.

"That's right," replied Kate. She explained how she
had learned to ride before she could walk. Everybody said
they'd never seen a little kid who was such a natural. By
the time she was five, she was entering children's

36

contests, and winning every time. At seven, she was preparing for trick riding. But that was before an accident in the barn.

"I didn't lose my ability to ride, mind you," said Kate confidently, "but not everybody agrees."

"You mean your dad?" guessed Megan.

"You got it," replied Kate. "I think he'd be happy if I sat on some satin cushion for the rest of my life and knitted, though I have a lot more trouble with needlework than I do with riding!" Then Kate grew more serious. "I really love my pa. He taught me everything I know. But he's wrong on this one."

"Can't you talk to him about it?" asked Megan.

"Oh, I've tried," replied Kate, sounding more and more frustrated as she went on. "I asked him to let me enter the wild west show this year. I can do trick riding with my eyes closed. . . ."

Megan and Kate laughed together at Kate's joke.

"I have a way of saying crazy things without thinking," declared Kate.

"I like the way you say things,"
replied Megan.

"Hey, you're a really nice person," said Kate. "Would you mind if I got a better picture of what you look like?"

"Well, I'm about your height . . ." Megan began, but

that wasn't what Kate had in mind.

Kate placed her hands on Megan's head, touching her hair, then her eyes. She used her fingers like a paintbrush, getting a sense of Kate's nose, then the shape of her face.

"You're prettier than me . . ." said Kate, "by a hair."

"Thanks." Megan laughed.

"I see well enough," said Kate firmly. "Being in Buffalo Bill's Wild West Show has always been my dream. But all I hear is 'Be careful, Kate.'"

"What about your mother?" Megan wanted to know.

Surely one of her parents would understand that Kate
was as capable as most kids with perfect vision.

"Ma tries to stand up to Pa. Usually he listens to her,
but not about me. You'd think I was made of glass."

"Isn't there anybody else who can help?"

"My older brothers used to treat me like one of them,
before the accident. I could always ride faster. I still
do, when Pa's not looking. They try to put in a good word
for me from time to time, but Pa won't listen to them
either."

"You have to find a way to make him listen," Megan
told Kate, remembering how her friends wouldn't take
her seriously. "Sometimes I have dreams that seem
impossible," she confided. "I get discouraged, too, but
I know I'll never stop trying."

Kate threw her head back and laughed. "I guess we're
a lot alike. We both have dreams. . . ."

By this time, Thunderbolt was well behaved and
walking calmly around the corral.

"Hey, boy!" said Kate, slapping him on the rump.
"You're getting pretty lazy. We need to make you kick up
some dust. What about it?"

"Anything in mind?" asked Megan.

"I've got an idea for a little exercise for all of us."
Some performers from Buffalo Bill's Wild West Show—

the biggest and most exciting show anybody had ever seen, Kate explained—were passing through the area on their way farther west. They had camped nearby to be close enough to give out the prizes at the wild west show that night.

"Our wild west show is really little compared to Buffalo Bill's, but the ranches around here have got the best riders anywhere," Kate bragged.

"Who's giving out the prize for trick riding?" Megan wanted to know, eager to learn more about the local show she was supposed to be in.

"Why, Annie is," replied Kate. "Annie Oakley."

Megan couldn't believe her ears.

"Don't just stand there," she told Kate. "Let's go!"

Chapter

Five

THE REAL ANNIE OAKLEY

K ate gave a whistle. It was strong and sharp, the kind of whistle her friends back home practiced and never seemed to get it right.

In a few seconds, a spirited horse about the same color and size as Thunderbolt came trotting over to the gate. When he spotted Kate, he stopped and waited patiently.

"That's Sparky," Kate told Megan as the two girls led Thunderbolt out of the corral. "He's my best friend."

Kate reached for a bridle as they neared the fence.

"Here, let me help you out." In one swift movement, she took the halter off Thunderbolt and slipped the bridle over his head and put the bit into his mouth. Then Kate tossed a saddle over his back. Megan watched as Kate fastened the cinch and checked the stirrups. "He's all set."

Megan thanked Kate and took the reins. "Was Sparky your horse before the accident?" Megan asked Kate.

"Sparky and I have been together since I was little. I tell him he's my first and last horse. Makes him feel special."

Then Kate told Megan how Sparky had become her eyes after the accident. She relied on Sparky and, together, they were a team.

"Did you ever compete on Sparky?" Megan asked.

"Oh, sure," replied Kate excitedly. "A lot of times. We used to be pretty good at any kind of racing. And we could be the best at trick riding . . . if somebody would just give us a shot at it."

"There must be a way," declared Megan. "You can't give up."

"You're right!" cried Kate, and she hopped on over Sparky's hindquarters the way Megan had seen stunt people do in the movies.

It was Megan's turn to mount Thunderbolt. She put her left foot in the stirrup and tried to remember all the things she had learned about riding. The next

thing Megan knew, she was on Thunderbolt's back.

"Pa's not real happy when I ride off like this," moaned Kate. "Let's not make a big fuss about leaving."

They waited until they were a safe distance down the dusty path before they broke into a trot. As Annie Oakley's camp got closer, Kate shouted, "Let's find out what Sparky and Thunderbolt can really do!" And with that, she kicked Sparky into a gallop that sent him flying off across a wide and grassy meadow. "Last one there's a rotten egg!" she shouted.

"Okay, boy," Megan whispered to Thunderbolt. "I'm ready if you are."

Thunderbolt didn't need a kick to understand. His gait immediately changed from a trot to a gallop. Megan gripped hard with her knees, held onto both reins, and kept her heels down. Megan was amazed when she stayed on without any trouble at all. In fact, the ride was smooth and even.

When the girls reached the crest of the last hill, Kate signaled to Megan to stop. "Shush," Kate said as she strained to listen. Megan heard the echo of gunshots in the distance.

"Are we in danger?" asked Megan nervously.

Kate laughed. "Of course not. I have a feeling that's just Annie Oakley practicing. You know, you're really funny sometimes!"

Megan hadn't meant the question to be funny. "Why do you think it's her?" she asked.

"I can tell by the fast and steady timing of her shots," declared Kate.

"That's amazing!" cried Megan.

"Well, don't be too impressed," Kate added. Then she confessed, "I also know that Annie Oakley's the only sharpshooter at the camp who'd be practicing that way—over and over again."

"I'm still impressed," replied Megan.

The girls dismounted and walked their horses. When they reached a clearing, Megan had a perfect view of the person doing the practicing. There stood the western star of Megan's books—Annie Oakley, the woman who had made history. She looked just like her pictures. The skirt of her long buckskin dress was neatly pleated. Around her neck, a starched ruffled collar looked newly ironed, though Megan wondered how anybody ironed their clothes in the Old West. Her hat had a narrow brim, probably so it didn't get in her way, and her long brown hair fell down her back gracefully. Everything about this star was perfect!

A row of dull brown bottles, made almost golden by the glow of the setting sun, were lined up on a boulder a distance away from Annie Oakley. Carefully and purposefully, she raised her rifle, sighted her target, and pulled the trigger. Time after time, the bottles broke into a thousand little pieces that sprayed glass high in the air.

"I can hardly believe that!" cried Megan.

"Wait," said Kate.

At that, Annie Oakley turned her back to her targets. Then she rested the rifle on her shoulder, steadying it with one hand. With her other hand, she held up a small mirror. A quick glance in the mirror was all she needed.

Once again, the great star hit the bottles every time.

"They don't call her a trick-shot and sharpshooter for nothing," declared Kate.

For the next few minutes, Megan and Kate sat under an outcropping of rocks, watching and listening to their own private wild west show.

When Annie Oakley had finished practicing, she emptied her rifle and started back to the camp.

"That was amazing!" exclaimed Megan.

The books Megan had read about Annie Oakley told about her incredible talent, but they also said she worked hard to make her dreams of fame come true.

"Can we meet her?" Megan wanted to know.

"We might meet her tonight," replied Kate. "We've got to get back. Besides, wasn't it enough to see her? It sure was enough for me to hear her. . . ."

"It was enough," said Megan.

Chapter

Six

IMPOSSIBLE
DREAMS

hen the girls arrived at the corral, Kate's father
was waiting by the fence.

"Better let that girl practice some," Sam Duffey told
Kate. "The hours are ticking away."

"I could get in some practice, too, Pa," pleaded Kate.
"A stand at a trot maybe. . . ."

"Now you know we've been through this before, Kate,"
her father replied. "Best you'd be getting on home to help
your ma."

Kate stood her ground. "Ma said I could stay for the wild west show."

"Don't much see the point. But have it your way." Sam Duffey's head hung low as he headed out of the corral.

"Come on," said Kate to Megan, tying Sparky to the fence. "Let's see what you can do."

I must have done this before, thought Megan. Otherwise, how can I trick ride Thunderbolt tonight?

Kate strapped a pair of chaps over her pants, and the girls led Thunderbolt to the center of the corral. He was still gentle and even-tempered. The bee sting seemed long forgotten. Kate put Thunderbolt's halter back on him and then strapped on his trick riding surcingle for Megan to hold on to.

"You know what to do," said Kate, holding Thunderbolt steady while Megan got on. Kate kept Thunderbolt on a longe line as Megan trotted him around the corral.

After a few minutes, Megan adjusted to Thunderbolt's gait and to riding without stirrups. She still didn't dare let go of the surcingle handles, though.

"Maybe you'd better give me some extra pointers on standing," suggested Megan.

Megan dismounted and Kate climbed onto Thunderbolt. She put him into a fast trot around the corral. Moving in perfect rhythm with the pony, Kate pulled herself into a kneeling position, holding tight to his thick mane. Then, in one quick motion, she stood straight and tall. Anybody who didn't know about Kate's blindness would have thought she was just another wild west show rider, and very talented for her age.

"They call this the crowd pleaser," Kate told Megan. Then she jumped off. "And it's so easy to do, too."

"Nothing to it," bluffed Megan, but her shaky legs told the truth.

"It's your turn!" commanded Kate. She helped Megan mount Thunderbolt and got him circling at a trot again on the longe.

Megan barely started to stand, but she lost her footing and slid right off Thunderbolt and onto the hard dirt of the corral.

"Ouch!" shouted Kate. "Even I felt that one."

"Ouch is right!" moaned Megan, rubbing a bruised spot on her leg.

Kate led the horse over to Megan. "Here, hop on. And remember to grab his mane tightly to steady yourself."

"Maybe I'm not ready to do this," replied Megan.

"We'll never know until you try," Kate told her.

So Megan eased Thunderbolt into a trot once again. Slowly, she kneeled, guiding him with the long reins.

"Now . . ." commanded Kate.

Megan took a deep breath.

"MAKE THE MOUNTAIN!" Suddenly Hannah Green's words popped into Megan's mind. How hard it must have been for Ms. Green to climb her first mountain or hang high above the earth with only a rope to keep her safe. She really was brave and daring. Megan knew this now more than ever. Finally, she let go of Thunderbolt's mane and slowly stood up straight.

To Megan's delight, she felt steady and sure of herself. As her fear melted away, she and Thunderbolt became partners. Around and around they went, Thunderbolt and Megan—smooth, confident, and perfectly balanced.

If only my friends could see me now, thought Megan, raising her arms high in the air.

"Maybe it's a good thing I'm not riding tonight. You might really show me up!" declared Kate good-naturedly.

Then the two of them led Sparky and Thunderbolt over to a shady tree to relax until it was time for the wild west show to begin. It was early evening, but the sun was still an orange ball blazing down on them.

"I'll get water for the horses," offered Megan.

When Megan returned with the water, she found Kate

strumming a guitar and humming softly. The guitar was made of a deep brown wood. Kate's fingers moved skillfully over the strings.

"It's beautiful," said Megan. "I'd really love to be able to play the guitar."

"It's easy. Here." And Kate showed Megan how to hold the guitar and strum a few simple chords. "Try 'Home On The Range.' It's the first song I learned to play."

To her surprise, Megan was soon playing and singing along. The strings buzzed a little as she stretched her fingers to play the chords, but the song still sounded okay. When she had finished, Megan laid the guitar carefully in its hard leather case, nestling it in the red velvet lining.

"You're so lucky to have a guitar like that," Megan told Kate, but Kate seemed to be off in a world of her own.

Megan touched Kate on the arm, and Kate jumped.

"Sorry," apologized Kate. "I was just thinking . . ."

"Thinking about what?" Megan wanted to know.

"You'll find out," replied Kate, a hint of mystery in her voice.

Chapter Seven

THE WINNER IS . . .

Megan signed up for the trick riding just outside the ring and drew number seven. She would be the last one to perform. Being last is good this time, thought Megan. I'll have a chance to watch how the other girls ride.

As Megan filled in the entry form, she heard the crowd groaning whenever a cowboy got thrown from his horse or steer, and cheering when a rider stayed on until the end. I'm paying attention to sounds more now because of Kate, thought Megan.

There were ponies and horses everywhere. Anybody who ever wished for a horse would be in heaven here, thought Megan. She couldn't believe how fancy the saddles were, trimmed in silver, gold, and precious stones. They looked more like works of art from a western museum, especially the saddles with intricate designs worked into the leather.

The crowd had really turned out. Most of the people, including the kids, looked just like Megan would have suspected. They wore jeans, western hats, and, of course, cowboy boots. Megan noticed that a few of the women and families had dressed up for the occasion. One woman wore a ruffled dress and carried a fancy parasol. "I decided to wear my Sunday go-to-meetin' clothes," Megan overhead her tell a friend.

People going in the opposite direction jostled Megan as she made her way toward Kate. As Megan walked closer, she saw that her friend was crying.

"What's wrong?" Megan wanted to know right away.

"I thought I could pull it off," sobbed Kate. "I walked right up to the judges bold as you please and told them I was there to sign up. They would have let me, too, but my father was standing close enough to hear me, so that was that. . . ."

"Maybe I could talk to him," suggested Megan, wondering how she could convince him when everybody else had failed.

"Thanks," replied Kate, "but it's too late."

All Kate needs is one big break, thought Megan. She's right about being able to ride as well as anybody else here. Her father just needs to see for himself. . . .

"Your father will change his mind. I just know he will. Besides, there are other wild west shows," Megan told Kate, trying to sound hopeful.

Another cheer went up from the crowd. A cheer like that could be for me tonight, Megan said to herself. Then she thought about how great it would feel to receive first prize from Annie Oakley herself.

"Sure, there are other wild west shows," said Kate, still fighting back tears.

This dream is important to me, thought Megan, but it's even more important to Kate. And I can make something happen right now. "Don't give up yet," Megan told her, giving her new friend a hug. "I've got an idea. Let's go get the horses."

A few minutes later, Megan and Kate were discussing a plan.

"The horses look so much alike that only an expert will notice it's Sparky," suggested Megan, pleased with herself.

"Like my father," added Kate.

"With luck, he won't know until it's too late to stop us," declared Megan.

"Are you sure you want to do this?" Kate frowned in concern. "*You* could probably be the best."

"This means more to you," replied Megan. "It's your only chance. I know now what I can do. And that's what counts. . . . Here, put this on," said Megan, handing her shirt and jacket to Kate.

"Hey, it's only the horse who's supposed to be bareback!" joked Kate as the girls traded clothes.

While they waited for the trick riding event to begin, they stood right next to the ring and watched the children's greased pig contest. Five piglets were let loose in the ring. A bunch of little children waited eagerly by the fence. Their job was to catch those piglets. The only hitch was that the chubby little animals were greased with lard.

Megan laughed as the children took off, grabbing one animal after another only to have each one slip from their arms, squealing and carrying on as the crowd cheered and hollered.

The trick riding came after that.

The first six girls were all good riders. When number seven was called, Kate turned to Megan. "You'll be at the start of my run, won't you?"

Megan had noticed that all the trick riders had somebody hold their horse and help get them started. That same person was there for them when they were finished. "I'll be right there," she assured Kate.

Megan led Kate proudly into the ring and then stepped out of the way.

Kate and Sparky went through their moves around the ring without a single flaw. Kate made her tricks look like play; her performance was perfect. Megan watched, proud that she'd been able to help make this happen. Still, she had to admit to a small twinge of regret. After all, she'd given up her only chance to ride in a real wild west show.

Out of the corner of her eye, Megan spotted Sam Duffey. The startled look on his face said that he had recognized his daughter. Would Sam dash into the ring and stop the competition? Megan held her breath. . . .

As Kate rode around and around the ring, her expression said, "I did it!" She waved over and over again, and the crowd sent up cheers that didn't stop. No wonder they called that trick the crowd pleaser. When Kate halted, people from all around ran up, congratulating her. Kate just couldn't seem to stop grinning.

Sam Duffey was clapping harder and shouting louder than anybody else. He clapped even louder when Kate accepted her prize from her hero, Annie Oakley—a pair of silver spurs and a new lasso.

"You were great!" cried Megan as Kate dismounted.

"Thanks, but I couldn't have done it without knowing you were there for me," declared Kate.

"I'm glad I was," said Megan. The way things had turned out made her feel warm all the way to her toes.

"Maybe you'll get a prize next time," suggested Kate. Then she thought for a second. "Or maybe we'll share it."

Kate handed Megan her prize spurs for a closer look. They were engraved with scrolls and flowers, and they shone like brilliant stars in a dark sky.

"I'm going to wear them when I do trick riding for Buffalo Bill's Wild West Show someday," declared Kate.

Although Megan laughed and talked with Kate as they exchanged clothes again, she realized that it was time to go home.

"You know, you helped me see things differently," Megan told Kate. "I'll never forget you, ever."

"You're talking funny now," said Kate, whose father was shouting across the ring that it was time to head home. The sun had set and most of the crowd had gone. Only the smell of settling dust and horses was left. They were smells that Megan would miss.

"Hey," called Kate, holding out her guitar to Megan. "I want you to have this. It's my thanks for what you did."

"I can't take your guitar!" cried Megan. "You'll miss it."

"I'd be happy knowing it's safe with you," said Kate.

Megan ran her fingers across the smooth wood. "It's wonderful, but I'll remember you without a present."

"Well, okay." Kate jumped on Sparky and gave him a gentle kick. "You take care now," she cried, and then she waved good-bye.

Megan was left alone by the side of the ring.

"Well boy," she told Thunderbolt. "Sure wish I could take you with me. We've got a nice garage. . . ."

Just then, Annie Oakley passed by. Megan noticed a small mirror in Annie's back pocket. It was the same one she had used during her target practice.

Megan was tempted to tell Annie Oakley how she'd read so much about her, but Annie Oakley would be very surprised that she was a heroine in popular books.

"Excuse me," said Megan instead, walking over to

the western star. "I wonder if I could borrow your mirror for a second."

Annie Oakley turned around. "Why sure," she replied, and she smiled. Then she handed her mirror to Megan. Peering at her reflection, Megan was surprised that her strawberry blond hair was brown now from all the dust.

As Megan wiped a smudge of dirt from her cheek, she heard the sound of a lawn sprinkler through a partially open window. Annie Oakley's little mirror had been replaced by the long one in the attic.

The sprinkler was watering Ellie's flowers. Megan was home again.

Chapter
Eight

BACK HOME

Ellie was in the kitchen fixing dinner, clanking the pots and pans as she unhooked the cookware from the rack above the old black stove. Then Ellie began to hum a cheerful tune and Megan started to hum along.

Kate had said her hearing became sharper after her accident. Maybe from now on, Megan decided, she would pay more attention to sounds and smells. It was funny the way you didn't give the sound of a pot much thought until . . .

Then Megan heard
Monty bark loudly. Few
people could miss that!
"Must be chow time at
the old corral," Megan
said out loud.

"Can you stay for
dinner?" asked Ellie.

Megan smelled
something roasting in the
oven—chicken maybe. It would probably be delicious,
but Megan was looking forward to having dinner with her
mother and Aunt Frances. "Thanks, but tonight the three
of us are having dinner together," she replied.

"Well, that's too good to miss. You know you're always
welcome to be my guest."

Megan knew Ellie was referring to dinner, but she had
a feeling Ellie also meant the attic.

"It's always special . . ." Megan began.

Megan pulled out a chair the color of the western
sunset and sat down. She had a few minutes left before
she had to be home, and she wanted to tell Ellie about
her adventure and how it had made her think differently
about a lot of things in her life.

"I know now that I can make my dreams come true,"

Megan said, munching on a carrot stick that Ellie had peeled just for her. "Even though my friends say I might not be able to."

"Your friends may be trying to protect you," replied Ellie. "Or perhaps they just don't yet understand how important your dreams are to you."

Right away, Megan thought of how Sam Duffey had tried to protect Kate.

Ellie went on. "You're the only one who can really make the difference."

"Make the mountain!" said Megan. "It's the motto of somebody I know."

"I'm going to remember that," said Ellie, whipping a little milk into the mashed potatoes.

"Ellie, sometimes I wish my friends thought the way you do," sighed Megan.

Ellie smiled at her. "They may when they've had a chance to think things over . . ."

The next morning before class, Heather, Keisha, and Alison were waiting for Megan on their bench outside the gym.

"We know you went to the attic," said Heather. "I called before dinner and Frances told us you were at Ellie's."

"Out with it!" cried Keisha. "We're dying to hear."

"What did we miss?" Alison wanted to know.

"For starters, you missed the most amazing, the most adorable, the fastest horse in the world!" Megan waited for their reaction. As she expected, Heather was the most excited. Next to Megan, she was the one who loved horses the best.

Saving the part about Annie Oakley until later, Megan told her friends about her adventures with Kate. They hung on her every word when she got to the part about the trick riding.

"I don't believe it!" cried Heather. "That's so great!"

"You really did that?" Alison wanted to know.

"I *really* did that," replied Megan proudly.

All of a sudden, everybody was talking at the same time.

"Okay, admit it," Megan teased her friends.

"Admit what?" Keisha asked. "What did we do?"

"Well, I know you didn't mean anything, but I was really upset that you didn't take my dream about becoming a diplomat seriously."

"You're right," replied Alison. "I started thinking about what you said after we all went home. And I guess I wasn't being fair." Heather and Keisha nodded in agreement.

"Thanks," said Megan. She was happy that her friends would admit this, but then, that's the way it was being good friends with Alison, Heather, and Keisha. They were always able to work things out.

Together, the four headed for class.

"Hey," said Megan as they started to file into the room. "Did I tell you about Annie Oakley?"

Kids were pushing past, trying to make it to class before the last bell. But Megan's friends stood frozen in the middle of the hall.

"I'll tell you at lunchtime," she teased.

As Megan headed through the classroom door, she wondered if maybe she'd be invited to their school one day as a guest speaker. If that happened, she knew *she'd* have lots to tell the class about making their dreams come true.

Diary

Dear Diary,

    I almost did it! I almost brought home a horse to live in our garage! Just kidding, but I really did get to ride the most wonderful horse named Thunderbolt. At first, he almost lived up to his name, but by the time the adventure was over, he should have been named Cupcake, he was so sweet. I still haven't given up my dream of having a horse, so I'll save the name. Maybe I'll buy a horse someday when I have my own career as a diplomat. That will make two dreams come true!

    I wonder what happened to Kate when she got home. I'll bet her mother and her brothers were proud of her. I could tell that Sam Duffey had changed his mind about what Kate could do. Kate might not be able to see, but she's not going to let anything stop her from being all she can be. I wouldn't be surprised if she becomes a wild west show star someday. Maybe she and Annie Oakley will meet again. I'd like to think so . . .

I looked up all the books on Annie Oakley in the school library today and a few about wild west shows. The bell rang and I didn't have time to check out the two I haven't read yet, so I'll do that next week.

When I told Ellie about the guitar, she suggested I learn to play it myself. I'm going to talk to Mom and Dad about taking music lessons with Ellie. They already know what a good teacher she is.

Well, Diary, it's time to get a little shut-eye. You sure got an earful this time, but when your dreams come true, you want to remember how you felt and save the feelings forever . . .

Love,

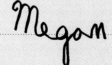